Kids love reading
Choose Your Own Adventure®!

"Getting to choose what path you take in books is fun. *Choose Your Own Adventure* books are so amazing for that reason."

Flora Esteban Hollister, age 10

"I have nev
books let m
than

Kyle Leighty, age

"They are super fun and super detailed!"

Ava Morey, age 9

"I felt like I was in the story."

Bridan Merrill, age 9

"I read them because they really hook me into them and it gives you choices. That way it takes you on an adventure and you don't have to read page to page."

Alannah Audet, age 11

"Sometimes you can't get sucked into a good book but these are amazing :)."

Kaiden Vernile, age 12

CHOOSE YOUR OWN ADVENTURE®

SPIES: MARY BOWSER

BY KYANDREIA JONES

ILLUSTRATED BY JASON MILLET
COVER ILLUSTRATED BY MIA MARIE OVERGAARD

CHOOSECO®
WAITSFIELD, VERMONT

Choose Your Own Adventure Spies: Mary Bowser
© 2020 Chooseco LLC, Waitsfield, Vermont. All Rights Reserved.

Book design: Stacey Boyd, Big Eyedea Visual Design

For information regarding permission, write to:

CHOOSECO
P.O. Box 46, Waitsfield, Vermont 05673
www.cyoa.com

ISBN-10: 1-937133-39-7
ISBN-13: 978-1-937133-39-9

Names: Jones, Kyandreia, author. | Millet, Jason, illustrator. | Overgaard, Mia Marie, illustrator.
Title: Spies. Mary Bowser / Kyandreia Jones ; illustrated by Jason Millet ; cover illustrated by Mia Marie Overgaard.
Other Titles: Mary Bowser | Choose your own adventure. Spies.
Description: Waitsfield, Vermont : Chooseco, [2020] | Interest age level: 007-012. | Summary: "YOU are Mary Bowser, a spy in Virginia. Freed from slavery, you have teamed up with Elizabeth "Bet" Van Lew to form a spy ring of powerful, brave women. You are as quick with your weapon as you are with your mind, and you work secret messages and poisons into everyday objects. Hidden in plain sight, you and your ring change the outcome of the Civil War"-- Provided by publisher.
Identifiers: ISBN 9781937133399 | ISBN 1937133397
Subjects: LCSH: Bowser, Mary Elizabeth approximately 1840---Juvenile fiction. | Van Lew, Elizabeth L., 1818-1900--Juvenile fiction. | United States--History--Civil War, 1861-1865--Participation, Female--Juvenile fiction. | Women spies--Virginia--Juvenile fiction. | Spy stories. | CYAC: Bowser, Mary Elizabeth, approximately 1840---Fiction. | Van Lew, Elizabeth L., 1818-1900--Fiction. | United States--History--Civil War, 1861-1865--Participation, Female--Fiction. | Women spies--Virginia-Fiction. | LCGFT: Action and adventure fiction. | Choose-your-own stories.
Classification: LCC PZ7.1.J722 Spm 2020 | DDC [Fic]--dc23

Published simultaneously in the United States and Canada

Printed in Canada

10 9 8 7 6 5 4 3 2 1

To Kale K who always cheers me on.
And to Jane who inspires me to
pursue my What Ifs.

Lastly, to Gib Gab, Willa, Betsy, Lizz, and
Cilly, for their friendship has deepened my
laughter, courage, and resilience.

BEWARE and WARNING!

This book is different from other books. YOU and you alone are in charge of what happens in this story.

Your name is Mary Bowser, and you are a free woman. You are fearless and strive for a better future for everyone. You can ride standing on the back of a horse while shooting a bow and arrow. You never go anywhere without your sword— named *Pointy*. You are an excellent spy in almost every way, but you excel at disguising yourself. This is why you are the perfect fit for this mission.

It is the middle of the Civil War in America and you are part of a spy ring made up of powerful and brave women. Although you have been freed, you want to remain in Virginia and fight for the freedom of other enslaved people. You go undercover in the Confederate White House, disguised as a servant, to spy on Jefferson Davis. Along the way you will encounter danger, friendship, and even magic! You will also make choices that will determine YOUR own fate in the story. Choose carefully, because the wrong choice could end in disaster—even death. But don't despair. At any time, YOU can go back and make another choice, and alter the path of your fate . . . and maybe even history.

You will not be bested by a tree. You tighten your grip on the willow oak tree's lowest branch, using your arms to pull your whole body up.

"You can do this," you whisper to yourself. Rain begins to fall. You wipe the moisture from your face. You can see the second story window slightly open just like you left it. As you reach up to grab another branch, you step on your long purple dress and your feet fly out from under you. Luck and your upper arm strength are all that save you from falling 70 feet to your death.

It is a wonder that women accomplish anything in this horrible garb, you think, sucking your teeth in frustration. This rainy summer night in Richmond, Virginia, is not the first night that you have had this thought. It is also not the first night that you have climbed this willow oak tree outside the Confederate White House.

The year is 1864, during the height of the American Civil War, and you are Mary Bowser, trained spy and the natural foe of every evildoer, villain, and criminal mastermind. For this reason, you were called upon by members of the Union League, an abolitionist secret society, to infiltrate the Confederate White House disguised as a servant in the household.

As a former enslaved person turned renowned spy, you were thrilled to spy on the President of the Confederacy, Jefferson Davis. You hope you can help to end this gruesome war.

Turn to the next page.

2

Every night you are able, you sneak out of the Confederate White House to meet your friend, Bet Van Lew. Bet advises you on your mission and shares all the intel that you have gathered on President Davis with the Union League. Bet is one of the smartest, fiercest, and bravest people you know. Bet has to be intelligent, powerful, and courageous because she is one of the few people in Virginia who is against the Confederates. You and Bet both take a great risk by meeting. Because you are not white like Bet is, the consequences if you are caught are much more severe.

But you are always careful. You sneak out of the house when everyone is asleep. This method has worked for you for the past three months that you have been spying. The only complaint that you have is the stubborn, enormous willow oak tree. You must climb it to return to your room on the second floor unnoticed.

Enslaved people are not allowed to wander around the White House grounds, and they are certainly not allowed to be out past curfew without the permission of President Davis.

You take the bottom of your wet, muddy dress and tie it into a knot, freeing your feet from the long, flowy material.

That should help, you think, wiping your muddy hands on the damp fabric. You hoist yourself up the last few branches until your hand clasps the wooden window frame.

Turn to page 4.

4

You crawl through the open window, entering the room feet first. Once inside the room, you close the window behind you and breathe a sigh of relief. You made it!

You are about to change out of your muddy dress when you hear the sound of someone striking a match. *Ppppppfffffffft*. The faint, warm glow of a candle's light illuminates the dark room. Your body goes cold. You are not alone.

You turn around to see another black woman standing in the middle of your room. It does not take long to recognize the short, full-figured woman, standing in her long white dress and white hair bonnet. Her name is Arena and she is President Davis's head house servant. Arena is the person that you answer to for all your chores and duties. You have always kept your distance from her because of her assertive, bossy attitude. You cannot avoid her now.

You stand frozen, feeling panic spread through your body. *What am I going to do? What will Arena think of me sneaking around at night? Will she tell President Davis? How do I get out of this?* you wonder. Your heartbeat drums in your ears. *BOOM BOOMPH. BOOM BOOMPH. BOOM BOOMPH.*

You are so overwhelmed with emotion that you almost do not notice the sword in Arena's hands.

Turn to page 6.

Wait a second. The bronze hilt. The six-inch smooth silver blade. The word *Pointy* etched into the central ridge of the sword . . . you know that sword. You look down at the floor where you hid your sword and suck in your breath at the sight of the missing floorboard. Oh no . . . Arena has found your secret stash! You stare at your black trousers, your black blouse, and your black boots—all the belongings that connect you to the spy world. Your diamond-encrusted mask rests on the floor too.

Adrenaline rushes through your veins. Suddenly, your arms are no longer tired from the 70-foot climb.

"Who are you?" asks Arena, breaking the painful silence. "I mean, who are you *really*? Why are you here in this house?" It is the worst question that anyone could ask a spy. If you tell Arena who you are, you will also have to tell her what you are doing in the Confederate White House. You could endanger your whole mission.

Go on to the next page.

But Arena *is* an enslaved person. There is a chance that she will keep your secret and support your mission. After all, the intelligence that you gather may be used to both end the war and abolish slavery. Why would she jeopardize the freedom that she would gain if you are left to your spying?

"If I were you, I would not lie to me," adds Arena, watching you rack your brain for a solution. "I may not have experience with this sword, but I do know which side is the sharp end."

If you answer the question honestly and reveal your secret, turn to page 9.

If you protect your mission and try to reason with Arena, turn to page 16.

You step away from the window and let out a breath. You keep an eye on your sword. Arena tightens her grip on the weapon when you move. You stay still, speaking in a steady voice in spite of the threat of impalement.

"My name is Mary Bowser, and I am a spy," you confess. You say your name with confidence and pride. Your name is known around the globe. You are one of the few spies who can shoot an arrow while standing on the back of a speeding horse. You are one of the few spies who can leave a battlefield unscathed—not a scratch on your skin. You are one of the few spies who can blend in anywhere, hiding under the cover of invisibility that your many disguises offer you. *That* is what made you the best person for this mission and *that* is what makes you qualified to handle this current dilemma.

Yet, Arena's face does not change at the mention of your name, or your job. There is no surprise or astonishment or even interest. Her face remains as unmoving and as calm as stone. Word of you and your reputation has not made it to the executive mansion.

Turn to the next page.

"One of my missions has brought me to the Confederate White House. It is my job to gather intel, or information, on President Davis and the Confederates."

"A spy? You aren't enslaved?" asks Arena. Something in her face brightens at her question.

"No, I am not an enslaved person," you answer. "I am free."

These words impress Arena. She takes a moment, sitting in the wooden chair by the door. She rests your sword on the wall behind her. Though the interrogation is not over, you have gained some of her trust. Arena motions for you to take a seat.

"If you are free," asks Arena, "why would you choose to live in the Confederate White House? You could die with your last moment on earth having been taking care of children that are not yours or cleaning dishes that you never got to eat off, surrounded by people who do not see you as a person."

Go on to the next page.

"I chose to disguise myself here," you say, answering Arena's first question, "because pretending to be a common servant is the best way to get close to President Davis. I value what is best for my mission and for my people."

The other answers to Arena's questions are more complicated. You watched the war and slavery destroy the bodies, the spirits, and the minds of your people.

Of course, you have considered the possibility that you could die in slavery. However, paying the ultimate price does not stop you from carrying out your mission. On the contrary, it is the risk and the fear that *all* black people could die enslaved that inspires you to give your mission your all and to see this war through to the end.

"You must be very brave," says Arena. "Most people would neither come back once they were freed nor look back at those they left behind."

"I am not most people," you say, holding out your hand to Arena. Arena grabs your sword from the wall and places it into your open hand. Thankful to have your weapon back, you hug Pointy close to your chest.

Turn to the next page.

12

You can tell that Arena would like to say more to you. You look down at your muddy dress and then at your inviting bed. You are exhausted from the night's events and you must wake up early tomorrow to report to your post. However, you are curious about Arena's secret. You have seen her burp babies, clean dishes, and wait on the Davises hand and foot. She is always working or barking orders. You have never seen her do anything else. How could she possibly have a secret and you not know about it?

If you decide to try to sleep and face things in the morning, go on to the next page.

If you ask Arena about her secret, turn to page 46.

After a restless night, you rise at dawn, returning to business as usual. Your spy kit is back in its place beneath the floorboard and you plan to push the whole ordeal with Arena out of your mind. You put on a long, beige dress, pulling your hair up in a burgundy handkerchief.

Like most days in the Confederate White House, you have much to do. Your daily duties consist of cleaning the house and tending to the Davis children under the direction of the housekeeper, Mrs. Mary O'Melia, and assisting the steward, Edward Eggeling, with the horses. The chores are grueling, but they give you a chance to study the innerworkings of the house. You learn a lot by eavesdropping on fellow servants.

Although your secret seems safe for now, you are not thrilled that you were discovered. You will have to work faster, beginning with choosing a productive start to your day.

If you start the day by making breakfast, turn to page 32.

If you start the day by cleaning the house, turn to page 39.

If you start the day by helping the steward, turn to page 44.

"Of course not. We are going to *ask* the tree to bring us down."

You are about to ask Arena what she means by asking the tree when she begins to sing softly:

Oh, Great Willow Oak,
please carry me down.
Carry me down to the ground
where I will stand safe and sound.
Oh, won't you please carry me down?

As Arena sings, the willow oak tree glows a faint purple hue. Its glowing branches reach through the window, encircling the woman's waist. The tree lifts Arena off the ground, tilting her with ease as it carries her out of the room. Even with its enormous branches, the tree is gentle as it softly sets Arena onto the ground.

Your mouth drops open. For three whole months, you have struggled to climb this tree and all you had to do was sing to it? That could have saved you a lot of time and work! Though, you admit that a glowing tree, however faint, is not very subtle.

If you choose to ride the magical tree, turn to page 51.

If you find another way out of the house, turn to page 59.

16

You must protect your mission at all costs. You take a step forward, hoping to reason with Arena. Your movement animates her. She springs into action, pointing the sword at your neck.

"Ah ah ah," warns Arena, holding the blade an inch away from your throat. "Not another step."

In the candlelight, Arena's face is still. Maybe she is bluffing. You stand tall, planting your bare feet onto the wooden floor. You feel mud squish between your toes.

"I knew something was strange about you from the moment that you stepped foot on these grounds," says Arena. "You are not who you say you are."

"Arena," you start, staring down the tip of your sword, "I am who I have been for the past three months: a hard worker, a loyal woman. Please put down the sword."

"Not a chance," retorts Arena.

Go on to the next page.

You sigh. It is hard to reason with someone when they have the upper hand. You are losing patience. You are exhausted from your climb and you would like to change out of the disgusting purple dress.

You watch Arena as her arm struggles under the weight of your sword. Though your sword is only three or four pounds, Arena has a hard time keeping it raised. It is obvious to you that she's never held one before. She clasps her hands over the hilt instead of gripping the handle as if she were shaking a hand.

As an expert swordswoman, you are confident that you could retrieve your sword from Arena. Or, you could simply move out of Arena's striking range so that you are no longer at risk of bodily injury. Either way, this ends now.

*If you choose to take back your sword,
turn to the next page.*

*If you choose to move out of striking range,
turn to page 54.*

18

You want your sword back. You duck under the blade and snatch the sword from Arena, clasping your hands around the hilt. You hold the sword with confidence, pointing it at Arena, who raises her arms in surrender.

"Not a step," you say, backpedaling to create distance between the two of you.

Arena does not listen to your command. She flings the door open and runs out of your room with a speed that you do not expect. She races into the dark hallway, disappearing around the corner. Wow, that woman can move!

You start to run after her, but you pause. You do not know the layout like Arena does. Arena has lived in the Confederate White House for years. She could hide in the building for days and you would not find her.

Though she does not know your true identity, Arena still poses a significant threat to your mission. What if she finds President Davis and tells him what she discovered? Leaving the Confederate White House while your identity remains intact might be the only way to salvage the mission.

You *have* successfully delivered three months' worth of intel. Two things are for sure: you cannot stay in your room and you are running out of time.

If you decide to leave the Confederate White House, turn to page 20.

If you choose to find Arena and stop her from revealing your secret, turn to page 26.

After three long months of spying, you decide you must leave the Confederate White House. You are determined to put some distance between yourself and the White House grounds. You quickly change from your muddy dress into the spy outfit Arena found beneath your floor boards.

You scale down the willow oak tree and enter the Virginia forest adjacent to the mansion. You are disguised in your diamond-encrusted mask as well as the rest of your spy gear. The black blouse, black trousers, and black boots suit you well.

You are thankful to wear a more comfortable and functional outfit. It is so much easier to run for your life in pants! You race through the forest with your sword, Pointy, strapped to your side.

There is no moon to guide you through the dark, but you run with ease. You have been trained for moments like these. You depend on the silhouette of the trees, keeping an eye on the long branches as you move deeper and deeper into the forest.

The ground is wet and slippery from the rain. There are rocks, logs, low-hanging branches, and other obstacles to beware. Yet, you run with precision and purpose, using the momentum of each trip, slipping and sliding to maintain your forward motion.

Go on to the next page.

You are not sure where you are going, but *forward* seems like a good start. You can't believe you must leave your mission behind. However, you cannot forget all that you have accomplished in your short time.

You have gathered and shared three full months of intel with Bet and the Union League. The Confederacy has had the same goal for the past three years: convince all the states where slavery is allowed to secede from the United States of America. They must also fight to protect and defend their territories from the Union Army.

In your last meeting with your friend Bet, you told her about President Davis's new war strategy called the *offensive-defensive* strategy. Facing declining resources and soldiers, Davis's new plan creates a flexible defense system that allows the Confederate troops to travel more and meet their military needs.

Because the Union forces have chosen an *offensive* strategy, invading the South and capturing territories, this last piece of intel is very useful. The Union Army may be able to execute a counterstrategy and turn the tides of the war.

Turn to the next page.

Of course, it is not enough just to receive the information. Union officials must do something worthwhile with it. You should return to Bet's headquarters and see how the Union League intends to use your intel! You have never played a role in what happens next. What if you could help the Union Army launch new missions and develop strategy?

You are about to change your course to Bet's headquarters when a bright, golden light in the distance stops you. At first, you fear that the light is the torch of a slavecatcher or an enemy solider, but you quickly realize that you are mistaken.

The light does not seem to be attached to anything at all. It spins, a sphere moving through the air. The mysterious, golden light illuminates an entire section of the forest, showing a small clearing between the trees.

"What in the world?" you wonder aloud, touching your fingers to your lips. You are not the only one who has taken an interest in the mysterious light. Several figures loom in the shadows.

Turn to page 25.

You head toward the light. You close your left hand around Pointy. You doubt that you could *fight* the mysterious golden light, but you feel better gripping your weapon. After all, the clearing is full of animals and you, for one, have no intention of being eaten by wolves. You watch as a pack of gray and red wolves files into the clearing, taking their place among the other woodland creatures.

To your relief, the wolves pay you no mind. In fact, all of the animals fixate on the mysterious light, circling around the strange force.

You walk farther into the clearing. As you approach, the light spins around and around. Finally, it settles, transforming into a large female bear. The bear stretches two feet taller than you, standing on its hind legs.

"Be not afraid," says the bear in a melodious voice. That is easier said than done. You notice the bear's concave face, her broad shoulders, and her short, round ears. Your eyes settle on her long, sharp claws.

Turn to page 66.

You recognize the outline of deer, raccoons, squirrels, and other woodland creatures—all heading toward the light.

The forest must be having a party, you think, taking in the strange scene. You are not sure if you want to be invited.

"Mary Bowser," says a voice. It is a soft, singsong voice and it seems to come from the light.

If you choose to head toward the light, turn to page 23.

If you stick to your original plan and return to Bet's headquarters, turn to page 70.

26

You have decided to find Arena. You must be cautious. You are taking a risk by leaving your room. The least that you can do is appear normal. This means no sword, no spy gear, and no muddy dress. You return your sword and the rest of your belongings to their place beneath the floorboard. You change into a clean beige nightgown and straighten the colorful handkerchief on your head. You blow out the candle before leaving your room.

An inexperienced spy might have raced after Arena without thinking, but you are not new to this game of pursuit. You tiptoe down the hallway, barely making a peep as you creep in the direction in which Arena fled.

Arena has a head start and she knows the Confederate White House better than you. You do not like being at a disadvantage. But it is in moments like these, when your adrenaline is rushing and your heartbeat is racing, that you do your best work.

Go on to the next page.

Portraits of President Jefferson Davis line the walls, watching you with beady blue eyes.

How many paintings does a man need of himself? you think. There are at least twenty portraits in this hallway and all of them depict President Davis in moments of thought, valor, or elegance. It is amazing that a man can be a hero in one community and a villain in another. The President Davis that you know is not so thoughtful, brave, or elegant. The President Davis that you know believes that slavery is fair, acceptable, and necessary. For this reason, you do not support images of him as anything but stubborn, misguided, and close-minded.

Turn to the next page.

28

You cannot shake the feeling that you are being studied, that someone or something lurks in the shadows, making note of your every move. Is this feeling a response to the night's strange turn of events? Or is that instinct locking you in place?

If you try to ignore the feeling and focus on finding Arena, turn to the next page.

If you decide to trust your instincts and stop pursuing Arena, turn to page 76.

Focus, Mary, you think, keeping your mind on the night's main objective. You must find Arena.

You listen out for the sound of footsteps or heavy breathing. It appears that Arena is not new to this game of cat and mouse either. You do not hear or see any signs of the woman.

You are about to descend the staircase when the *click* of a bedroom door catches your attention. *Gah!* Someone is coming! You press your body against the wall, keeping very still as candlelight pours from a nearby room. You stare down at the shadow stretching into the hallway. You hold your breath. Of all the doors in this hallway, of course, the one that opens is that of President Davis!

Go on to the next page.

First Lady Mrs. Varina Davis's sharp footsteps interrupt the noiseless hallway. *Tap. Tap. Tap.* Mrs. Davis must be looking for her husband. Why else would she roam the hallways at night? It is only a few hours until sunrise. Everyone is supposed to be asleep!

The tall, pregnant woman steps out into the hallway belly first. She makes her way to the wall of portraits, pausing at the largest one. She looks to her left and then to her right. You are grateful that there is no natural light to expose your side of the hallway. Mrs. Davis cannot see you. Sweat dribbles down your temple, your armpits, and your lower back.

The large portrait seems to have Mrs. Davis's undivided attention. This could be your only chance to escape.

*If you choose to sneak away,
turn to page 63.*

*If you stay and see what Mrs. Davis is up to,
turn to page 78.*

You start your day by making breakfast. You enter the Victorian-style kitchen, admiring the emerald, baby blue, and gold furniture. Despite the kitchen having a stove, two wooden tables, and three cabinets, the room feels spacious and comfortable. You grab a pot from the shelf and walk over to the stove.

You are in the middle of making porridge when a tall, short-haired woman walks into the room. You listen to the familiar, sharp *tap tap tap* of Mrs. Mary O'Melia's shoes against the wooden floor. She enters the kitchen without a word.

Mrs. O'Melia is a quiet but stern woman. She takes pride in her work as the housekeeper, keeping the kitchen in a pristine condition and tending to the Davis children. Mrs. O'Melia is in charge of maintaining the entire house as well as keeping all the house servants in line.

"Good morning, Mrs.," you say, grabbing four bowls from the cabinet. Mrs. O'Melia looks at you with her sad, round eyes, mumbling what you assume is a hello.

Turn to page 34.

You listen to Arena and flee the forest. *Crack! Crack! Crack!* You stay low, avoiding an unfortunate run-in with one of the Minni balls. Adrenaline keeps you on your toes. You race to the stables behind the Confederate White House.

You lock eyes with a brown American Standardbred horse that whinnies in your direction. You place a saddle on the horse's back and the bridle around her head. "Ready for a little fun, ol' girl?" you ask the horse. You open the stable door and hop on her back in one swift motion. You click your teeth and thrust your legs forward, racing in the direction of the gunfire.

You come up behind the cavalry men, taking your sword, Pointy, from your side. You stand tall on the horse's back as she speeds toward the three men who are all dressed in Confederate uniforms. They seem to be the only ones here. They must have been scouting out the area when they heard you and Arena in the forest.

"Drop your weapons and do not turn around or I will spill your blood where you stand," you command the men, wielding Pointy. The men do not hesitate, promptly obeying your orders. They put down their rifles before running frantically into the forest. You let them go, sitting back down on your new horse and returning to an injured Arena.

"I said do *not* be a hero," sighs Arena. She tries to sound irritated, but you can hear a smile in her voice. You return the grin, carefully lifting the woman onto your horse. You are not being a hero. You are just being Mary.

The End

34

Mrs. O'Melia's eyes have been sad ever since she left Ireland and came to the United States with her two small children. Having already lost her husband, Mrs. O'Melia was devastated when the war separated her from her children.

That is the harsh truth about war—it does not only harm soldiers. Mrs. O'Melia is one innocent victim among millions who have suffered because of this gruesome war. All the more reason to do your job well and put an end to the fighting.

The Davis's four young children will be downstairs shortly, so you take your mind off Mrs. O'Melia and set one of the wooden tables. You pour the finished porridge into four bowls and pull out the chairs just as Maggie, Billy, Jeff, and Joseph come running into the room. The kitchen awakens with their lively conversations, freeing you from the somber mood that Mrs. O'Melia brought with her.

"Porridge! Porridge! Porridge!" exclaim the children, sitting at the table. They are about to dig into their breakfast when you interrupt them with a look.

Turn to page 36.

"Have you washed your hands?" you ask.

"I washed mine," says the eldest, Maggie. Jeff and Billy also show their clean hands to you as proof. You look at the youngest, Joseph, who takes a sudden interest in his porridge. You take a soapy rag from the sink, bending down near the youngest of the Davis family.

"You must keep your hands clean," you remind the boy, cleaning his chubby little hands with the rag. "You cannot hold your little baby brother or sister with dirty hands."

The First Lady, Varina Davis, is pregnant with her fifth child, and the children have been over the moon about having another addition to the family. Your comment excites them, beginning their daily debate.

"I hope mommy has a girl!" says Maggie, swallowing a spoonful of porridge. "It is about time I have a sister."

"I hope she has another boy," says Jeff, "because boys are better!"

"I hope the baby is healthy and happy," you say before quieting the children. "Eat up so you can grow big and strong."

Go on to the next page.

You look over to see Mrs. O'Melia staring tearfully at her feet. She rubs the back of her hand across her face. The gesture does not stop the rivers from flowing down her cheeks.

"Are you all right, ma'am?" you ask.

The woman shakes her head, causing her curly brown hair to fall around the sides of her face. The children happily eat their porridge while you console the housekeeper. You hand Mrs. O'Melia a cloth to dry her eyes.

"All this talk of babies and new life and family!" cries Mrs. O'Melia. "My heart aches for my own children, but there is much work to do today. General Lee will be here any moment and I can barely collect myself. How am I supposed to make the proper preparations? Who is going to get the apple pie from the baker in town? Who will ready the library for the General's arrival?"

Turn to the next page.

38

You are careful to keep your face masked with concern rather than excitement about this new information. Confederate General Robert E. Lee is coming to the Confederate White House? *The* Robert E. Lee, Commander of the Confederate Army?! Imagine what you could learn if you were in the same room as General Lee and President Davis! You can hardly contain your excitement. You bite your bottom lip to keep from squealing with joy.

Control yourself, Mary, you think to yourself. *Act normal.*

*If you prepare the library for General Lee,
turn to page 82.*

*If you get the apple pie from the baker in town,
turn to page 84.*

You start by cleaning the first floor of the executive mansion. You dust and polish the furniture, tidy the kitchen, and change the living room curtains. You are in the middle of washing the great big living room windows when Arena approaches you. She wears a long navy-blue dress and a white bonnet on her head. A worried expression furrows her usually expressionless face.

"I have been up all night," says Arena. You do not react to Arena's comment. You take out another soapy rag and make circles on the windowpane. You do not have time to hear about Arena and her poor sleeping habits. Everyone is working right now except for Arena.

Someone important is coming to visit. It must be a high-ranking Confederate officer because you saw Ruth, one of the servants, polishing the Davis's best silverware and fanciest plates. You need to be ready for whoever is about to enter those front doors.

Turn to the next page.

"You must listen to me," says Arena. Her shoulder brushes yours as she fixes her gaze forward. She looks out the window and into the front lawn of the executive mansion. Her eyes widen. "Trouble is coming."

You follow Arena's gaze. Your smile drips from your face like sweat. A band of horse-drawn carriages and men on horseback approach the Confederate White House! You watch the sea of gray uniformed men ride by, numbering in the hundreds, but it is the man leading the Confederate soldiers who catches your eye. He rides a gray American Saddlebred, maintaining excellent posture as he races forward on his horse. His white beard and short white hair frame the look of determination and pride on his face. His gray uniform, the bright red sash around his waist, and the magnificent sword with golden ornate scabbard and handle make him look like the subject of a painting.

You were wrong. You and the other servants are not preparing for just any high-ranking officer. You are preparing for *the* most important officer, the Commander of the Confederate States Army, General Robert E. Lee!

Turn to page 42.

42

"We need to get out of here," says Arena, nearly stumbling over the furniture. You grab her wrist to keep her from toppling over the armchair.

"We must remain calm," you whisper, putting a hand on either side of Arena's shoulders. "We must not give him or his soldiers the satisfaction of instilling fear in us. We must act as though their presence does not rattle us. We must keep our heads. We must calm our breath."

"How do you do it?" demands Arena, watching as the Confederate soldiers reach the executive grounds. "How do you stand here and act as if the sight of them does not boil your blood? Think of all the lives that have been lost! Think of what they fight for! You should leave with me now. They are going to get what is coming to them."

Before you can react to Arena's words, Mrs. O'Melia and a train of the other servants march toward the front doors. With the other servants distracted by the arrival of the guests, Arena heads in the opposite direction.

You are supposed to greet the soldiers with the rest of the servants. Where in the world is Arena going? And what did she mean when she said that the soldiers are going to get what is coming to them?

If you follow Arena, turn to page 89.

If you greet General Lee with the other servants, turn to page 92.

"Why don't you want me to meet the Union League?" you ask Bet, leaning back in your chair.

There is no anger in your voice, only curiosity. Bet knows you as well as anyone. She has seen firsthand all the fighting, the spying, and the negotiating that you have done throughout your career. She believes in you. If she hesitates to set up a meeting between you and the Union League, she must have a good reason.

"They will not take you seriously," sighs Bet. She takes a moment to tidy her desk, awaiting your reaction. You help her neatly stack pieces of parchment. What does she mean that they will not take you seriously? The members of the Union League have taken your intel seriously. How are you any different?

"I will bring my sword then," you joke, watching Bet return the stacks of parchment to their respective hiding places around the room. "Pointy is quite persuasive."

"Oh, I know," says Bet, letting out a half-hearted laugh. "It is only that I do not feel comfortable sending you to Philadelphia. The Union League is not merely a boy's club, it's a lion's den."

"What is a lion's den to a lion?" you ask, refusing be talked out of your decision. If Bet won't introduce you, you will find your way into this den.

The End

44

You find President Davis's personal steward, Mr. Edward Eggeling, near the stables. He does not react to you. Instead, he stares fondly into a puddle, admiring the reflection of his fitted black coat, gray trousers, and long, rubber boots.

The horses neigh gleefully in their stalls when they see you. You sometimes visit the stables when you sneak out at night, feeding the horses stolen apples and brushing their long, luxurious manes. It calms you to tend to these beautiful creatures and to imagine you are riding them. It has been ages since you have ridden a horse.

Though you do not regret your decision to spy from the Confederate White House, it is not easy to sacrifice your freedom. Moments spent with these horses make your job bearable.

Mr. Eggeling, on the other hand, makes your time at the executive mansion more difficult. You expected this mission to demand more from you than any other mission. You *are* spying behind enemy lines. It is not easy to live among the enemy, and Mr. Eggeling is one of the most insufferable men that you have ever met. He is in love with himself. As you walk deeper into the large wooden stables, Mr. Eggeling continues to admire his reflection, shifting his attention to his sharp jawline and round, green eyes.

Turn to page 47.

46

As a spy, you know that secrets are currency. You have given Arena one of your secrets, your true identity, and now it is time for her to match your price. Whatever her secret is, it must be big. Just as you are more than what you seem, it is apparent to you that Arena is more than the head house servant. After all, who thinks to check under the floorboards when a servant goes missing? Arena must have been suspicious of you long before tonight. If this is the case, it is even more impressive that Arena had the patience to wait three months to act.

"Is there something that you would like to share with me?" you ask.

"Yes, but not here," responds Arena, before adding, "and change into your other clothes."

While you dress in your all black getup and diamond-encrusted mask, Arena walks over to the window and opens it. The rain has calmed down while you have been talking. The willow oak tree stands in all of its 70-foot glory. Arena looks at you, nodding toward the tree. You snort. She cannot be serious.

"You want me to climb back down the tree?" you ask, folding your arms across your chest.

Turn to page 14.

"Good morning, sir," you say, fixing your gaze on the horses rather than on the man in front of you. You lock eyes with a brown American Standardbred horse that whinnies in your direction.

"Grab a shovel and clean up this manure," responds Mr. Eggeling, pointing to the mounds of horse dung that rest in each stall. You are familiar with the tone of disgust in his heavy German accent. He speaks to everyone this way, but especially to those in the house who look like you.

"Are you too dumb or too simple to understand what I said?" asks Mr. Eggeling, watching you pause beside the wall of shovels. You lower your eyes, fighting to keep your cover.

I am smart enough to understand that dumb and simple mean the exact same thing, you think, gritting your teeth and grabbing a shovel.

Mr. Eggeling speaks to you like you are small. Like he could lift his leg and stomp you under his rubber boot if he so pleased. That is a brave way to speak to someone with a large, rusty shovel in her hands, who is not afraid to fight.

Turn to the next page.

48

You tighten your grip on the shovel as you slam it into the stinky heap of manure, holding your breath. The smell is horrible, but you focus to distract yourself from Mr. Eggeling's rude comments. You cannot stand bullies. It is a wonder that Mr. Eggeling has escaped the sharp end of your sword over these past three months.

Go on to the next page.

Mr. Eggeling, and others like him, talk to you like you are small and weak and dumb. Would a small person be able to stand tall in spite of being belittled, badmouthed, and bullied? Would a weak person be able to shoulder the weight of a divided country? Would a dumb person be able to gather intelligence right under the Confederacy's nose?

If you gave in to people like Mr. Eggeling, you would not have lasted three months on these grounds. But as a spy, you've learned techniques to keep your mind sharp and keep stress from overwhelming you. You can use one of these methods to cope and rise above Mr. Eggeling's attitude.

*If you go to your happy place,
turn to page 94.*

*If you console yourself with the truth,
turn to page 98.*

There is a first time for everything. You sing the song and climb back onto the branches of the magical tree. You hold tight while the glowing branches guide you to the ground.

How incredible is it that magic existed here all this time, and you only learned of it this evening? You glance back at the enormous tree. Its branches have stopped glowing, and yet you know its truth. A feeling of excitement washes over you. You bathe in possibility. It is reassuring to know that you live in a world with a little magic! Because of the war, you were beginning to believe that the world was mostly death and destruction.

Arena gestures for you to follow her into the woods near the executive mansion. With little warning, Arena dashes forward, racing through the trees. The ground is wet from the rain, but you are able to keep up with the alarmingly fast 60-year-old woman. When you reach a clearing in the forest, Arena faces you and hands you her white bonnet.

"Tie this over your eyes," Arena demands. You do what she says and tie the fabric over your eyes, and then Arena leads you deeper into the slippery dark forest.

Turn to the next page.

52

The night sky is a spilled bottle of ink when Arena removes your blindfold. The air remains thick with the moisture of rain. Against this dark, inky silhouette of night, you can see an old, decrepit church standing in the middle of a cornfield. The rusty railing curls off the porch and the screen door bends at a slant. The windows are boarded up. No light escapes from the church. Either no one visits this building or those who do are careful not to be seen. Nevertheless, there is relief on Arena's face when she sets eyes on the creepy, humble structure. Your face, on the other hand, registers both fatigue and confusion. Is this where Arena's secret lies?

"Is this place haunted?" you ask Arena, getting the heebie-jeebies. The stench of moldy wood wafts in your direction.

"Depends on your definition of a ghost," answers Arena, knocking twice on the screen door. Well, that is not a no. You would have preferred a simple no.

A child appears in the doorway. Candlelight shines behind her, sending warm light to your feet. She is barefoot, wearing only an old, dark green dress. *Creakkk* goes the rusty screen door as the child lets you and Arena inside the church.

Turn to page 55.

54

You decide to move out of striking range. You take a step back toward the window. The action startles Arena. She pushes the sword closer to you. You deflect the blow from your neck, causing the blade to fall onto your right foot.

Ouch! You bite down hard on your bottom lip to keep from screaming. Warm tears stream down your face as dark red blood trickles onto the wooden floor. You stare down at the sword, sticking out of your foot. Arena's eyes widen at the sight of blood.

"I said not another step," says Arena, releasing her grip on the weapon. Not another step is right— your foot never recovers from your injury.

The End

The abandoned church is filled with women and children taking shelter in every pew. The long benches are covered in tattered quilts, a few articles of clothing, and other humble belongings. As you make your way down the aisle, you meet the brown, green, blue, and gray eyes of many onlookers.

Your shoulders tighten with sympathy at the sight of the onlookers. Their faces look tired and worn. You suspect most of them are the family members of fallen soldiers. You recognize the look of loss, despair, and fear in their wide, sunken eyes.

Your eyes travel to other people in the room. Unlike those who wear dresses, blouses, trousers, and coats, the formerly enslaved people are still clothed in the tattered rags of their past.

If living people could be ghosts, then these women and children haunt this building. Their sadness chills your bones, reminding you of the harsh realities of this war: no one really wins wars as gruesome as this one.

Turn to the next page.

56

Everyone in the room takes notice of your arrival. Your ears pick up the whispers of people trying to figure out who you are and why you have come. To be fair, you *are* armed and wearing an all-black outfit and a diamond-encrusted mask. You would stare at you, too.

"Where is your mother, Avery?" Arena asks the gray-eyed child. Suddenly, the front door opens again.

A tall, blonde-haired woman dressed in brown trousers, brown boots, and a black hood walks into the room. The woman drags two dead animal carcasses behind her. She pulls the animals by the legs, wordlessly bypassing you and Arena. She hands the creatures to Avery saying, "See to it that the children eat first."

"Yes, mother," says Avery, soundlessly taking the animals and leaving the room. Noticing you at last, the woman turns to you and drops her hood.

Turn to page 58.

58

You notice the hunter's scar first. It is a thick mark that snakes from her left ear to her jaw. It is a fresh injury. Maybe only a few weeks old. The flesh is still scabbing over, healing from whatever trauma it endured. Arena clears her throat, giving you a warning look. You stop staring.

"Valerie, I have brought someone who may be able to help our cause," says Arena. You shift your attention from Valerie's scar to her gray eyes. Valerie holds your gaze, her eyes narrowing to slits.

"Our cause does not need help," snaps Valerie, looking from your black boots all the way up to your diamond-encrusted mask, "and certainly not from someone like her."

Someone like you? What does that mean? You try to conceal your offense, never being one to reveal when you are rattled. You look around at the people in the room. They watch you and Valerie with concern. You could do a lot of good here, but you must earn their trust and respect. Valerie for some reason has taken a dislike to you. Maybe if you can make her understand what you've done and who you are, she will be less suspicious?

If you apologize to Valerie and begin again, turn to page 99.

If you ask Valerie what she means by someone like you, turn to page 102.

A glowing tree is not subtle at all. You would rather find another way out of the mansion. Now comes the hard part: getting out of the house without being detected. Everyone should be asleep, but you can never be too careful.

Unfortunately, your spy gear is about as subtle as the magical tree. You have to take the chance. At least your blouse, trousers, and boots are black. The dark colors should help you blend into the dark hallway. You blow out the candle and sneak out of your room.

Once in the dim hallway, you press your body to the wall. You do your best to avoid the many portraits of President Davis. A miscalculated move causes your shoulder to collide with one of the old wooden frames. A portrait nearly falls, but you catch it before it hits the ground. Wow! That was a close one!

A bead of sweat trickles down your temple as you hold your position. You return the painting to its place on the wall, ignoring the rush of panic drumming inside your chest. *BOOM BOOMPH. BOOM BOOMPH. BOOM BOOMPH,* pounds your noisy heart. Between Arena giving you a fright and this close call, the poor thing is having quite the night. You might want to turn back and take the tree after all.

---

*If you decide to take the tree after all,
turn to page 73.*

*If you shake off your panic and continue with
your plan, turn to the next page.*

60

You shake off the panic, tiptoeing toward the winding staircase. You take the stairs two at a time, moving fast and with precision. A few more steps and you will be outside with Arena.

I can do this, you think to yourself. This is the same phrase that you whisper to yourself each time you climb the willow oak tree. This is the same phrase that you say to yourself when villains surround and outnumber you. This is the same phrase you breathe when you fight sleep as enemies creep in the night. You say, think, and believe this phrase because you understand that what you tell yourself in moments of doubt, distress, or fear is important. You must constantly encourage yourself to do the impossible and the extraordinary if you wish to survive the inconceivable and the incredible.

Your self-assurance pays off. You practically run to Arena when you make it outside. Arena's mouth drops open when she sees you. You smile at her in triumph. Way to go! You successfully escaped the Confederate White House!

Turn to page 62.

"I did not think you were going to make it out," admits Arena. "Why didn't you take the tree? Is the world-famous spy afraid of a little magic?"

"I am not afraid," you say, looking over your shoulder to make sure that you were not followed. There is no sign of anyone watching you from the house. Surprised by your good fortune, you breathe a sigh of relief. "Sneaking out through a door seemed like a better decision than taking a glowing tree."

"Are you not the least bit curious as to why the tree glows?" presses Arena, astonished that you have yet to ask her about the magical willow oak tree.

If you prefer to keep the tree's magic a mystery, turn to page 64.

If you ask Arena why the tree glows, turn to page 111.

You sneak away from the hallway, leaving Mrs. Davis with the large portrait. You tiptoe down the winding staircase, carefully taking the steps one at a time.

When you step onto the cold wooden floor, a loud *crash!* startles you.

That must be Arena! You run into the kitchen, looking for any sign of her. There is glass all over the wooden floor. A chair has been thrown through one of the kitchen windows. Why would Arena do such a thing?

You are not the only one who heard the noise. You see the scarlet of a candle's flame as footsteps approach the kitchen. You hide in one of the cupboards, closing the wooden doors behind you as the steward Mr. Eggeling and First Lady Davis rush into the room.

"Would you look at that!" exclaims Mrs. Davis.

"It looks like someone has escaped," says Mr. Eggeling. "I will sound the alarm and check every bed. Once we have a name of our missing person, I will ready the dogs. I assure you, Mrs. Davis, whoever it is will not get far!"

If Arena really wanted to escape, she could easily walk out of the front door or simply open the window. The only explanation for Arena throwing the chair through the window is that she wanted to make it *look* like someone was running away. A realization dawns on you from your place in the cupboard: Arena has set you up!

The End

You know better than to pull on loose string. If you untie the world's fragile fabric, your whole understanding of life could unravel. Some mysteries are better left unsolved. You are more interested in Arena's secret and where it will lead you. Leaving the White House grounds, you accompany Arena into the deep dark forest.

"I am more curious as to why I must leave the house to hear about your secret," you say.

"You will understand when we get there," replies Arena. It is clear to you that she won't budge, and you sigh at her stubbornness. You must be patient.

You listen to the forest's gentle melody, hearing the *ribbet ribbet ribbet* of frogs and *chirp chirp chirp* of crickets. A wolf howls in the distance. The sound of the animals causes you to reach for your sword Pointy, but the wolf is at least four miles away. The more pressing threat is the smell that has entered your nostrils.

Beneath the prevailing smell of rain, you recognize the stench of gunpowder. The smell of sulfur is so strong that you can't inhale deeply. The odor takes you back to the time before you accepted this mission. You remember your life before you infiltrated the executive mansion. You often disguised yourself as a male soldier, delivering intel to Union officials who fought valiantly on Southern territories. You recall the bodies and the battle cries and the painful sound of gunshot whizzing through the air. The rotten egg smell does not bring back fond memories.

Go on to the next page.

"We need to take cover," you say to Arena. Before you can explain yourself, the sharp *crack* of an infantryman's rifle echoes through the forest. You cover Arena's mouth to keep her from screaming.

The tree a few feet away from you erupts with Minni balls. *Crack! Crack! Crack!* Pieces of bark fly all around you. You've got company and they are armed to the teeth. You press your belly to the ground. Another round of Minni balls passes dangerously close to you. You hear an *oof!* as Arena falls beside you. She has been hit!

"Save yourself," instructs Arena. She holds her arms against her abdomen. Dark red blood stains her white dress. You look into her dull blue eyes and apply pressure to the wound.

"Don't be a hero," she insists. "Save yourself and complete your mission."

If you decide to listen to Arena and flee the forest, turn to page 33.

If you do not listen to Arena and try to carry her to safety, turn to page 104.

66

"You have nothing to fear," she insists. "My name is Bala, Goddess of Confidence and Fearlessness, and I am here to guide you."

A goddess? What would a goddess want with you? You are just a spy, a great one, but a spy nonetheless.

"You are more than great," says Bala, reading your mind. "You are extraordinary."

When she speaks, you hear music. It is a sweet, drawn-out note in a soulful ballad. She looks at you with her soft, black eyes. You can see why the animals are in awe of her. There is a softness and a fierceness to her that you admire.

"I know you inside and out, forwards and backwards, upside down and right-side up," continues Bala. "I know your past, your present, and your future too. I am here to guide you and see to it that you are successful in achieving your destiny. I want nothing more than to watch you change this country for the better, first by bringing an end to this horrible war."

Bala opens her giant furry paws, showing you the truth in her words. You see images of yourself in her palms. You stand, sword drawn and valiant on the back of a speeding horse. You rise from battlefields without a scratch on your skin. You hide in plain sight, blending into your surroundings like a chameleon. You cannot help but smile at these images of who you are and of who you will become.

Turn to page 68.

"Wow," you say, watching your life unfold in Bala's palms. She smiles a wide, sharp-toothed smile.

"You may summon me at will," says Bala, already beginning to fade. "All you have to do is think about a moment in which you were fearless or confident and you will have my full force and might."

With these incredible words, Bala transforms back into light. She disappears into the night sky, coloring the horizon in the orange, pink, and yellow of sunrise. What a night!

Go on to the next page.

Your mind returns to the plan that you had before your encounter with the Goddess Bala. Now that you have the support of a fierce magical being, you feel more confident to advocate for yourself and your skills. You can be more than a spy. You can play a role in what happens with the information you gather! You could discuss war strategies with the Union League, or you can discuss them with Union General Ulysses S. Grant himself. You may even be able to bring your ideas and fresh perspective on the war to President Abraham Lincoln!

After meeting the Goddess Bala, you are not afraid to dream. The only question that remains is just how big will your dreams become.

If you decide to discuss war strategies with the Union League, turn to page 106.

If you choose to discuss your intel with Union General Ulysses S. Grant, turn to page 109.

If you bring your ideas and perspective to President Abraham Lincoln, turn to page 112.

You have learned the hard way not to walk toward bright lights and singsong-y voices, but that's a story for another time and place.

You stick to your original plan and return to your friend Bet's headquarters. Bet is surprised to see you, but she respects your decision to leave your post at the Davis home.

"It would have been catastrophic if I lost my finest spy in that miserable house," says Bet before adding, "not to mention the heartbreak that I would have sustained if I lost my dearest friend!"

The two of you are in Bet's two-story mansion, sitting in her parlor. Bet sits at her oak desk in a sky-blue dress that complements her bright blue eyes. Her long blonde hair is up in a bun, keeping the strands out of her face. Encrypted letters take up a large portion of the desk, piling as high as the ceiling.

"I was hoping to last longer than three months!" you scoff.

Bet smiles and says, "You have done well in your three months. You should be proud of the intelligence that you gathered."

"About that," you say, recalling your plan to discuss war strategies with the Union League. "I would like to sit down with the mysterious Union League and discuss the intel that I shared with you last night. The strategies are complex, and I believe that it would be beneficial if I explained it to them myself."

Turn to page 72.

Something shifts in Bet's face at your words. Her lips become a thin line. She places a hand under her chin, mulling over your request. You can tell she does not like your idea.

"I apologize," says Bet, realizing that she has offended you. "I have a lot on my mind. Maintaining a secret spy network is not easy. Especially recently, with the name-calling and the threats and the Confederate spies following me everywhere I go—"

"Name-calling? Threats? Spies following you?" you interrupt, bewildered.

In all your meetings, Bet has neglected to mention any of this important information. With the possibility of Bet being in danger, your plan to discuss war strategies with the Union League does not seem as pressing. Though the timing of this crucial information seems rather convenient if you do say so yourself . . .

If you think it's important to switch your attention to Bet and her potential problem, turn to page 74.

If you'd rather try to find out why Bet does not want you to meet the Union League, turn to page 43.

Suddenly, the magical tree seems worth the trouble. You walk back into your room and close the door behind you. You open your mouth to recite the song:

Oh, Great Willow Oak,
please carry me down.
Carry me down to the ground
where I will stand safe and sound.
Oh, won't you please carry me down?

In response to your singing, the magical tree glows its faint purple hue, but its branches do not reach out toward you like they did to Arena. Instead, the tree's colors become more vibrant, practically erupting in violet. Though you do not speak "tree," you understand the gesture. The willow oak tree does not like being your second choice.

You stare at the willow oak tree, a new irritation growing between you and your nemesis. In all fairness, if you *did* ask the tree a question, there was always a possibility that it would say no.

The End

You switch your attention to Bet. Every day, the world sees a relentless, determined, and contemporary leader. You see a stressed and overworked person, your dear friend, sitting in her place.

Here in the well-lit parlor, you notice the signs of stress that have been difficult to detect during your nighttime meetings. There are bags beneath Bet's eyes from sleepless nights. There is red around her fingernails from her anxiously biting them. You consider, too, the piles of paper everywhere. Bet's parlor has never been this disorderly. She usually tucks all evidence of her spy network in secret compartments and drawers and underneath floorboards. If anyone entered her house at this moment, they would be suspicious of the piles of encryption-covered parchment.

"There is so much that you could do," says Bet, interrupting your revelation. "I need someone to travel to Philadelphia and train new spy recruits. Someone must go to The Vegetable Farm and lead a new task force to help soldiers who are wounded or in distress. I have countless missions in Maryland, New York, and Vermont that only someone of your expertise could handle."

You detect a pattern in Bet's plans for you: they all involve you traveling far from Richmond. Why is Bet trying to get you out of Richmond? And does it have to do with whatever trouble she is keeping from you?

Go on to the next page.

Since you were a child, Bet has protected you and cared for you. She has never treated you differently because of the color of your skin, believing in your right to compassion, fairness, and freedom.

Rather than driving a wider wedge between the two of you, the Civil War has strengthened your bond. If Bet needs you, she will have your support whether she wants it or not. Friends are always there for each other and you intend to remind Bet that you are there for her.

If you pretend to accept a mission but really spy on Bet, turn to page 117.

If you decide to ask Bet what is going on, turn to page 120.

76

You trust your instincts and stop pursuing Arena. You cannot shake the feeling that you are being watched. You stand still. You squint your eyes to better assess your surroundings. You make out a tall figure standing menacingly on the other side of the dark hallway.

"Heh heh heh," says a voice, covering your skin in a fresh layer of goosebumps.

You recognize that creepy, low chuckle. It belongs to President Davis's steward, Mr. Edward Eggeling. He is responsible for maintaining the White House grounds, tending to the horses, landscaping, and upholding the respectable appearance of the executive mansion. During the past three months that you have been spying in the Confederate White House, you and Mr. Eggeling have crossed paths several times, and each encounter has been increasingly unpleasant.

"What are you doing out here?" questions Mr. Eggeling. It is too dark to see his face. However, you can hear a smile in his voice. He approaches you slowly, moving like a shadow. You move too, backpedaling one foot at a time.

"You are out past curfew, Mary," says Mr. Eggeling. "What do you suppose President Davis will have to say about that?"

Go on to the next page.

You do not intend on finding out the answer to that question. Between Arena fleeing and being discovered by Mr. Eggeling, this whole night has been a disaster. You could cut your losses and make a break for it. Though a feeling of defiance comes over you as you stare down Mr. Eggeling's menacing silhouette. You resent the way he walks toward you, like a lion stalking a gazelle. You, Mary Bowser, are not prey.

If you decide it's time to take down Mr. Eggeling, turn to page 124.

If you choose to make a break for it, turn to page 126.

You fight the urge to sneak away, remaining on your side of the dark hallway. You do not have to wait long to see why Mrs. Davis has taken an interest in the large portrait. She puts both hands around the right side of the portrait's frame. With a sharp and deliberate tug, Mrs. Davis pulls the frame toward herself and disappears behind the painting. *The portrait is a door,* you realize.

You give Mrs. Davis a head start before you follow, counting to 500 in your head. When you finish counting, you slip behind the portrait and take the colorful handkerchief from your head. Your curly hair falls below your neck. You quickly put the damp fabric in between the frame and the wall, preventing it from closing completely. This is not your first secret passage and you refuse to be trapped forever behind this creepy painting.

After you have secured the doorstop, you turn in the direction that Mrs. Davis walked. You listen to the *tap tap tap* of Mrs. Davis's footsteps as she storms down the passageway. It is too dark to take in your new surroundings.

How can Mrs. Davis walk with such confidence in this pitch-black passageway? you wonder, running a hand along the cold, damp wall. Your fingers close around a rope attached to the wall. Ah ha! The rope makes traveling in the dark easier! You feel Mrs. Davis pulling on the rope. Tug. Tug. Tug. You touch the rope lightly, using it to guide you deeper into the passageway.

Turn to page 80.

Within a few minutes, the rope ends and you near a well-lit room. You are in a study, housing over a thousand books, a wooden desk, and a map of the Confederate territories pinned to the wall.

In the middle of the room, Mrs. Davis sits on top of an oak desk. Her eyes are fixed on the entryway and her arms are folded across her chest. She wears a fresh smirk on her face. *For whom is she waiting?* you wonder.

"I know you are there, Mary," says Mrs. Davis, answering your unspoken question. "Come have a chat."

How could she possibly know that you followed her? There is only one way to find out. You step away from the dark hallway and cautiously approach the First Lady.

"You are a Union spy," states Mrs. Davis, watching you carefully. It is not a question, so you remain quiet, staring back at the pregnant woman. "Do not fret. I am on your side."

"I have some information that may help your cause," continues Mrs. Davis, ignoring the look of shock and confusion on your face. "The Confederates have been struggling against the Union Army at the Siege of Petersburg. I am certain that General Lee will abandon Richmond and Petersburg completely if he keeps losing supplies and men. If you send word to General Grant to apply *more* pressure to the Confederates, Lee will give up and irreversibly tip the war in the Union's favor."

Go on to the next page.

"Why would you tell me this?" you ask. "Why would you go against President Davis?"

"A woman ought not share everything with her husband," replies Mrs. Davis. "I never believed in this war and it is about time that it has ended."

"But what will happen if people ask you about all this?" you ask. "What will you say if I'm caught, and they ask you if I was spying under your nose?"

"I will say that I never heard of you," says Mrs. Davis, not missing a beat. "Hurry along now, the sun will be up soon, and you have a job to do."

You can barely contain your shock. You cannot fathom how Mrs. Davis discovered your deepest secret. Before you exit the passageway, you have one last question to ask: "How did you know?"

"The woman of the house rarely misses anything," chuckles Mrs. Davis. "You can only scale a 70-foot tree so many times before someone sees you. Very impressive, by the way."

Years after the war has ended, many reporters ask Mrs. Davis if she ever suspected that there was a spy living alongside her. They speak of you, Mary Bowser, and true to her word, the former First Lady denies that the two of you ever crossed paths. But you will never forget that fateful day in the Davis's secret passageway when you realized that you and Bet were not the only women in Virginia who were against the Confederates.

The End

You prepare the library for General Lee. You dust the bookshelves and straighten the furniture. You bring a pot of tea and a platter of cornbread into the room. You set it down as President Davis and General Lee walk into the library, speaking quietly to each other.

General Lee catches your eye. You recognize him by his familiar white beard. He wears his gray Confederate uniform. There is a bright red sash around his waist and the magnificent sword with golden ornate scabbard and handle. President Davis stands beside the general, dressed in his finest clothing, a classic black suit. The two men look like subjects of a painting as they sit down across from each other, drinking tea and eating the cornbread.

They continue their conversation as if you are not there. You listen closely. They discuss the trench war in a city just south of Richmond called Petersburg. You already know something about this. The Union General Ulysses S. Grant created long, narrow ditches, or trenches, surrounding the city after he failed to overtake it. His soldiers fight from those trenches and the warfare has been deadly.

Go on to the next page.

"My men are doing their best to defend Petersburg and Richmond," says General Lee, "but we must acknowledge that the numbers are not in our favor. General Grant can afford to lose soldiers, whereas we simply have none to spare."

"What are you proposing?" asks President Davis, leaning forward in his chair. "Do we need more men?"

"More men," mutters the general, sipping his tea, "or less war."

"You are a fine general," argues President Davis. "Surely there is more to be done to keep control of our territory?"

"Mr. President, it is a matter of resources. Grant's army is . . ." General Lee is about to continue his sentence when he takes notice of you standing silently beside President Davis. He gives you a distrustful look before cutting through you with a single word.

"Leave," he says, watching you promptly exit the room. *Gah!* So much for spying on the infamous Confederate general!

The End

"I would be happy to help, ma'am," you say. "I will collect the apple pie from the bakery in town."

"Oh, wonderful!" exclaims Mrs. O'Melia. She nods her head toward the door. "Make haste! I would like to have the apple pie set out this afternoon!"

"Yes, ma'am," you say, barely containing your excitement. Your hand rests on the doorknob. Wait a second . . . You have never before run an errand that requires you to leave the Confederate White House. You do not know where the baker is or if you, as a black person, will be able to walk into the shop freely. The last thing you need is to run into trouble.

"Ma'am," you say, addressing Mrs. O'Melia, who has begun to order the other servants to prepare the library for guests. "Where may I find this bakery? Will anybody else accompany me?"

Go on to the next page.

"The bakery is next to Billups Funeral Home," answers Mrs. O'Melia, shooing you out of the room. "You must go around the back because you are not allowed to enter through the front. There is no need to knock on the door. The baker, Mr. Townsend, will be able to see you from the window. When he asks what you are doing on his back porch, tell him that you have come for an apple pie for President Davis."

Turn to the next page.

86

A few hours later, you are on your way back from the bakery when you get the feeling that you are being followed. It is a familiar feeling that raises the hair on your arms and neck. You suddenly feel foolish for taking a lonely dirt road as a shortcut to the executive mansion. You were focused on getting the pie back to General Lee and President Davis. You forgot that unfrequented roads are perfect places for spies and thieves to ambush unsuspecting travelers.

"My missus will be expecting me," you say to the hidden adversary. You stop in your tracks and hold the fresh baked apple pie in your hand like a weapon. The pastry is no Pointy but is all you have to defend yourself.

"Will she?" asks a familiar voice from behind you.

You turn to see a dark-haired, well-dressed Northern woman wearing shiny shoes, standing on the lonely dirt road. Her pearl necklace and earrings gleam in the sunlight. She holds her emerald dress in one hand and a golden dagger in the other. She may look like a fairytale princess but there is no villain more sinister than the one standing before you.

Turn to page 88.

"Emerson Weinberger," you say, addressing your archnemesis with a bewildered expression. You have not seen her since the war broke out. You have not seen most of your old enemies. With the war going on, there has been no need for villains.

"I bet you are wondering why I am here after all this time," says Emerson, with sinister smile. "I got a delicious little thought when I saw you in town. What better moment to take down the great Mary Bowser than in the middle of a war?"

"I hope you like apple," you respond, throwing the pan of pie directly at Emerson's smug face.

I am going to need a lot more than pie, you realize, watching Emerson skillfully duck out of the flying pastry's path.

The End?

With everyone in the Confederate White House distracted by the guests' arrival, you decide to follow Arena. You have to lift your hem and jog in order to keep up with the small woman. Arena heads through the empty kitchen to the back door. She swings the door open and races into the yard.

"Where are you going?" you ask Arena. You shield your eyes. The sun is bright this morning and there is not a cloud in the sky. You are thankful that everyone in the house is preoccupied. It would be hard to explain what you and Arena are doing outside.

"Arena, where are you going?" you ask again, running to grab hold of her. Arena looks down at your hand clutching on to her dress sleeve. You let go of her and clear your throat. "Arena, what is going on?"

Turn to the next page.

"Quit your yammering and keep up," responds Arena in the assertive, bossy voice you've endured the past three months. "We have to get as far away from here as possible."

You are about to challenge Arena's command when the smell of gunpowder stops you in your tracks. It is a familiar and overwhelming scent that reeks of rotten eggs.

You scan the backyard for the smell's source. You intuitively look toward the house, wondering if the soldiers brought the horrible odor to the executive mansion. You would not be surprised if the men's uniforms still carried the stench of war. But then, you notice figures lurking at the edge of the trees near the White House grounds. One blink and you might have missed the people disguised in the hunter green, brown, and beige of the forest.

"Arena," you say as a bad feeling settles in the pit of your stomach. Is this the secret that Arena wanted to tell you last night? While you do not know the exact reason these people are here, the smell of gunpowder does not make you think that they have come to break bread with the Confederates.

"They are not here for you. They are here for those men inside that miserable house," says Arena, turning to you at last. "They are here to end the war that brought violence, cruelty, and pain to this land, the war that claimed their loved ones, the war that left us to rot."

Go on to the next page.

"This is not the way," you argue, standing firm in your place. "There has been enough bloodshed in this war. You saw how many soldiers rode here with General Lee! These people in the forest do not stand a chance against them! They are more skilled, more organized—"

"Do not insult us," interrupts Arena. "You may be willing to ignore what these men have done, what their cause has done, but I will not. My army is smarter and mightier than you think. Even if we are not victorious, the Confederates will feel our strength."

"Must one always demonstrate strength with brute force?" you counter. "Show them that you are strong enough to find another way—one that will not end in the same chaos and carnage!"

"If you are not going to join us, step aside, Mary," says Arena, gesturing for you to move out of her way. Though she stands before you with an entire army behind her, you must not let her pass. You stare back at her, clenching your fists and setting your jaw in defiance.

"I will not repeat myself," warns Arena, recognizing the look of determination that covers your face like the finest armor. "You are either on our side of the war or theirs."

The End

92

You decide to greet General Lee with the other servants. You stand between the housekeeper, Mrs. O'Melia, and a servant named Ruth. You hold a platter of cornbread in one hand and a pot of tea in the other, offering the soldiers food and drink as they enter the mansion.

"Welcome, gentlemen," says President Davis, descending the winding staircase with Mrs. Davis on his arm. The two wear their finest clothing: a classic black suit for the president and a brilliant white dress for the first lady. All eyes are on them as they make their way down the steps.

"Top of the morning, Mr. President," says General Lee, shaking President Davis's hand. "While we are honored to be here, my men and I cannot stay long. We are still defending Richmond and Petersburg from General Grant's advances."

"Let us take this conversation to my library while your soldiers fill their bellies, General," offers President Davis. He releases his wife's arm and leads General Lee toward the staircase.

You are about to come up with an excuse to accompany the men when movement outside catches your eye. You walk over to the window, staring wide-eyed. Women and men race from the trees, carrying weapons. Arena is leading the charge.

"We are under attack!" you yell, pointing toward the window. Some soldiers unsheathe their swords while others take out their rifles at the sight of the mysterious army.

Go on to the next page.

"Under attack?" questions President Davis, looking pale from his place at the foot of the stairs.

"We will fend them off," declares General Lee. His soldiers abandon their food and drink. They rush out of the house to meet the army before they reach the executive mansion. *Crack! Crack! Crack!* The sound of gunfire shakes the house.

"I must get my family to safety," says President Davis. Mrs. Davis calls her four children, who hurriedly descend the stairs and run into their mother's arms, frantically asking, "Who are these people? Why have they come?"

"They are no one and they are here for nothing," answers General Lee, unsheathing his sword. President Davis gives General Lee a look of panic.

General Lee continues, "No one must learn about this, or more armies like this one will rise up. My men and I will handle this in secret and then return to the trenches in Petersburg. Leave now, and after we handle this, you must return here as if nothing happened. The last thing we need is to undermine your leadership with a scandal."

"You there!" shouts Mrs. Davis, pointing at you. You are frozen, shocked by the turn of events. "You heard the man! We must leave at once! Help me with the children!"

The End

Once Mr. Eggeling leaves the stables, you set down the shovel and close your eyes. You breathe in and out, listening to the calming sound of the horses whinnying from their stalls beside you. The *hee hee hee* of the horses guides you away from the stables, away from the Confederate White House, and away from this gruesome war. Suddenly, you do not smell the awful stench of horse manure or feel the rough calluses on your palms or hear Mr. Eggeling's impolite comments.

In your mind, you are riding a horse once again—a black stallion that you have named Phoenix. You wear your black blouse, black trousers, and black boots but you no longer need your diamond-encrusted mask.

Go on to the next page.

Your handkerchief keeps your long curly hair out of your eyes and frames the look of triumph and joy on your face. You emerge from the death and destruction unscathed, sheathing your sword Pointy to your side.

You have just left your last battlefield and you are riding valiantly away from the final scene of war. The war has ended and, with its end, slavery has also become a scar of the past.

Turn to page 97.

You picture perfectly the relief that you will feel once the Civil War has reached its end. Despite the hardships in the United States of America's past, you are excited for the country's future. You cannot wait to witness your former enslaved people take their rightful place as fellow citizens of this land. You look forward to the day that all Americans lean into a brighter destiny where everyone can live in harmony and treat each other with kindness, consideration, and respect. Freedom is the sweetest dream that you have ever dreamt and a promise that you are eager to fulfill.

With freedom still lingering on your mind, you dare yourself to open your eyes and pick up the shovel again.

Although life after the war does not exactly resemble your happy place, you and your friend Bet continue to impact your community and country in positive ways. You become a schoolteacher in the state of Georgia, helping freed black people become socially conscious, educated members of society. As for your good friend Bet, President Ulysses S. Grant awards her the esteemed position of Postmaster of Richmond. In her role as a postmaster, Bet creates a more efficient and modern postal system that employs newly freed black people until she retires in 1877.

The End

You will not be bullied into becoming someone that you are not. Let Mr. Eggeling believe that you are beneath him. You know that you are not small, weak, or dumb. You are the great Mary Bowser, world-famous spy and the natural foe of every evildoer, villain, and criminal mastermind. You may have spent the past three months disguised as a servant, but you cannot forget all the skills you have, and who you really are.

It is in your power to call off this mission and return to your friend Bet. You could put this war behind you and begin anew somewhere that accepts free black people, like Vermont or Canada. However, giving up is not in your nature. You have never run from a challenge; you have never backed down from a fight, and you have never left anyone behind. You do not plan on adopting these bad habits now.

With these positive thoughts in mind, you rise above your unfortunate interaction with Mr. Eggeling and all the other challenging moments that have occurred during your time in the Confederate White House.

Centuries after you have successfully completed your mission, you are celebrated in history classes around the country. Historians, teachers, and students alike rejoice that an individual like yourself existed and helped make the United States of America a better place. After all, you were an extraordinary person during a period in which slavery and war made monsters out of many people.

The End

"I think we are misunderstanding one another," you say to Valerie, taking off your diamond-encrusted mask. "Shall we begin again?"

"Very well," sighs Valerie, watching you with her intense gray eyes. You nod a thank-you before addressing both Valerie and the people in the pews. "It was not my intention to offend you. I realize that it is both useless and insulting to convince you that I know what is best for any individual in this room."

"That is right!" agrees someone in the crowd.

"Precisely!" shouts another.

"I will say, however, that I have seen a lot of chaos and carnage throughout this war," you admit, recalling every battle you have fought, every enemy you have slain, and every moment in between. "I wish only to support your cause and to do my part in ensuring that you all live to heal from your suffering."

Turn to the next page.

"We may not wear a fancy black suit and fancy mask or have a shiny, pointy sword," says Valerie, "but we are capable of fighting our own battles. There is not a person in here who has not experienced 'chaos and carnage,' as you call it. We will find our relief once we get revenge on those who caused our suffering."

"An eye for an eye!" cheers an onlooker.

"A tooth for a tooth!" yells another.

"So, blood begets blood?" you counter, shaking your head in disapproval. "Vengeance will not put food in your bellies or clean the residue from your skin or clothe your bones when they are cold. All vengeance will do, all vengeance can do, is send you to an early grave."

"And I would be the last person to say that you lot are incapable of defending yourselves," you add, nodding toward the many onlookers. "Some may look around this room and see victims, but I witness warriors. I spy survivors. I look upon those who survived slavery, and those who are surviving this war one day at a time, and I marvel."

"If you plan on leading with revenge," you say, "Valerie is right in saying that your cause does not need help from someone like me. Someone like me would find a better way to repay those who wronged me rather than to die with hatred in my heart."

Go on to the next page.

"And what better way is that?" asks Arena, finding her voice in the matter.

"You could join my spy ring," you respond, holding up your diamond-encrusted mask, "and fight your battle with full bellies and mended hearts."

Arena, Valerie, and the rest of their group accept your offer, deciding to join the spy ring instead of carrying out their plan to attack the Confederate White House. You make good on your promise, giving them access to the food, the clothing, and the shelter that they were denied.

The End

"What do you mean you do not need help from someone like me?" you ask, offended.

"Someone who sees themselves as a hero," retorts Valerie, pulling off your mask, "and everyone else as the people who need saving."

"I could be an asset to your cause," you argue, unflinching. "You would not have to hunt for food anymore or hide out in this church. I could guide you north where you would receive the aid you deserve."

"Do you think that we would blindly follow you out of the city that we have called our home?" huffs Valerie. The onlookers murmur their agreements.

"A *home*," you say, focusing on the particular word Valerie used to describe Richmond, "provides comfort, warmth, shelter. Look at you. You are sitting in an abandoned church that reeks of death. You are making blankets from rags and food from scraps. Surely, Richmond is not a home to you now?"

"You dress like a warrior," says Valerie, disagreeing with your statements, "but when you speak of fleeing, you wield a coward's tongue."

Go on to the next page.

"I am speaking of survival," you respond, appealing to the other individuals in the room. "Would you rather cling to the Richmond of the past than to embark on a new, bright future somewhere else?"

"This war has taken everything from us," says Arena, cutting into the heated debate between you and Valerie. "If we leave now, we leave as victims. We would rather leave as victors."

These words excite the onlookers, sending the room into a frenzy. You are not able to talk them down. You start to leave, but several onlookers block your path. They look at Valerie, awaiting her command.

"I am afraid you know too much," sighs Valerie, running a finger across her throat.

The End

104

"No one gets left behind," you say, deciding not to listen to Arena.

You pull the handkerchief off your head and then you do the same with Arena's. You use the pieces of fabric to secure the small woman onto your back. You place Arena's arms over your shoulders, ignoring the sticky feeling of blood seeping into your black blouse. More Minni balls whiz past you. *Crack! Crack! Crack!*

Tree bark flies this way and that. *Crack! Crack! Crack!* The gunfire is too close for comfort. You feel a sharp pain in your left thigh, but you fight the urge to cry out. The last thing you want to do is give away your exact location. You grit your teeth and stay low, rapidly crawling out of the forest.

You reach your friend Bet's headquarters, grateful that she does not live far from the Confederate White House. You knock on the door until your knuckles ache. Suddenly, the door flies open and Bet stands in the doorway with a loaded rifle in her hands.

"Oh, Mary," says Bet, setting down the weapon. Her expression changes as she notices the unconscious woman attached to you. You untie Arena from your back just before you collapse at Bet's feet.

Go on to the next page.

"Arena!" you yell, waking up with a start.

You are in a bed in Bet's attic. Bet has converted the attic into an infirmary. There are medical supplies and a tray of food by your bedside. Sunlight enters the room from a small window, signaling a new day. A raging pain in your left thigh reminds you of yesterday's events. Images of the last night bombard you. The dark forest. The flying pieces of tree bark. The silhouette of Bet's familiar two-story home. You look down to see that your left leg rests on a pillow, elevated and bandaged.

Arena lies in the bed to your right. Her white dress has been replaced by a shawl and black trousers. A bandage covers her entire torso. You look at her stone-like face. She does not seem to be moving.

"Arena," you say softly, fearing the worse. "Aw, Arena."

"Quit your whimpering, child," grumbles Arena, startling you. "I am trying to rest!"

"You gave me such a fright!" you say, letting out a nervous laugh. Arena turns her head toward you. Her expression is full of warmth and gratitude.

"Good," jokes Arena, smiling a wide smile, "that will teach you not to mind your elders."

The End

106

After your inspiring encounter with Bala, the Goddess of Confidence and Fearlessness, you head to Philadelphia to discuss war strategies with the Union League.

The members of the abolitionist secret society initially do not take you seriously. They are unaccustomed to taking suggestions from a woman and former enslaved person. However, it is impossible not to hear you out when you have good suggestions and when a magical being stands by your side.

You discuss how to get the most out of the intelligence that you gathered while hiding in plain sight as a worker in the Davis home. You all sit at a large round table. The elite group of men listen to your explanation, and then you begin discussing counterstrategies to Davis's offensive-defensive approach.

You understand that cutting off the Confederate troops' supplies would weaken their forces faster than occupying their southern territories. Rather than attacking these armies head on, you and the Union League plot that it would be best to go straight for the Confederacy's artilleries, food sources, and travel roads.

Turn to page 108.

"How are our soldiers supposed to get close enough to compromise the enemy's supplies?" asks Joseph, one of the members of the Union League.

"That is a good point," comments another member named Michael. The others in the room reluctantly murmur their agreements. They avoid contact with the grizzly goddess to your left. You look at Bala, who nods at you, urging you to continue.

"Your men cannot," you answer matter-of-factly. "We would not send in soldiers to sabotage the Confederacy's supplies. We would send in spies."

The End

You head south toward Petersburg, Virginia, where Union General Ulysses S. Grant and his Union Army are fighting in the trenches against Confederate General Lee's forces.

You disguise yourself as a male soldier. You don a navy Union uniform and crawl through the trenches to find the general. This is not the first time that your spying has led you to the front lines. You have brought General Grant intel before.

Despite your familiarity with the Union General, General Grant is difficult to spot. He wears a black civilian hat, muddy boots, and a modest, navy private's coat. You almost crawl past the bearded, dark-haired man. Thankfully, you observe the general's rank stitched above his elbow on his right sleeve.

Turn to the next page.

"Mary!" greets General Grant when you assume your place beside him in the long, narrow ditch. "Welcome to the happiest place in all the land!"

"General, I come bearing news," you say to him, grabbing a rifle and returning enemy fire. The memorable *crack! crack! crack!* sounds as bullets whiz through the air.

"What did you say?" asks the general, barely hearing you over the gunfire.

"I said, 'I come bearing news!'" you shout, cupping a hand around your mouth.

"What was that?" questions the general. It is much too loud to hear anything.

This is impossible, you think. You close your eyes and recall a moment in which you were fearless. Suddenly, a spherical ball of light appears before your eyes. It spins wildly until the Goddess Bala stands tall in front of you.

"RAWR!" roars Bala, causing every man to cease firing. A silence rests in the trenches. On both sides of the line, soldiers stare wide eyed at the giant bear standing in the narrow ditch.

"Mary," whispers General Grant, gawking at Bala, "you do know that there is an animal standing right beside you."

"Yes, she is with me," you say, setting down your weapon. "I come bearing important news."

General Grant chuckles at your pun before realizing that you are being serious.

The End

You give into your curiosity, asking Arena, "Why does the tree glow?"

To your horror, your question animates the tree. It grabs hold of you, engulfing you in its magical branches. You are blinded by a vibrant purple light as the great willow oak responds to your question by singing:

> *If you want to know why I glow,*
> *you need only believe*
> *in magic.*
> *A world without wonder?*
> *A world without mystery?*
> *Oh, surely that would be tragic!*
> *But all the more so,*
> *is to be left here to glow.*
> *Shall we trade places?*
> *I like to wear faces!*
> *You shall know my truth*
> *and I shall live yours,*
> *wearing pretty dresses and fighting with swords.*
> *You will unravel like a mystery*
> *and I will be you and go down in history.*

The End?

112

You arrive outside the presidential mansion in Washington, D.C., several weeks after your encounter with Bala. You plan to share your ideas and fresh perspective with President Abraham Lincoln. You are in the middle of climbing through the sixteenth U.S. president's bedroom window when a loud scream cuts through the quiet peace of the early morning.

"Please do not be Lincoln," you whisper, pushing aside the floral white curtain leading to the presidential suite.

Instead of the president, you find an empty bed with sheets strewn on the floor. A black top hat lays on its side. Your conversation will have to wait. President Lincoln has been abducted!

You drop down from the second-floor windowsill with Pointy in hand. The steel shines in the sunlight. You head in the direction of the scream, curious who would dare to kidnap a president in broad daylight.

You find three men on a dirt path secluded from the rest of the White House grounds. You spot two men wearing gray trousers, gray hoods, and black boots. President Lincoln kneels before them. The president wears a long, white night shirt, confirming that he was, in fact, stolen from his sleep. Though he kneels before these men, you can tell that he is a tall, mighty, and courageous man. He holds his head up, seeming to ignore the fact that there is a rifle pointing at him. The three men are having a heated discussion. You use their focus on each other as a chance to close in on them.

Go on to the next page.

"You should have never become president!" says the man holding the weapon.

"This country will be better off without you," agrees another critic.

"You can end my life," says President Lincoln without a trace of fear in his voice, "but you will never destroy my legacy. The strong foundation of liberty on which this new nation is built shall live on long after I have become dust."

"Save your breath," says the armed man. "There will be no need for speeches where you are going."

"I beg to differ," you interrupt. You clasp a hand on the assailant's elbow and thrust it upward, disarming him with a simple move.

"What—" he objects, staring at you wide eyed and confused. You quickly silence him with Pointy.

"You should not have done that," growls the man's partner, pulling out a curved blade. "You have no idea who you are up against."

"I can say the same for you," you counter, shielding the president with your body. The second man falls faster than the first.

Turn to the next page.

You help the president to his feet. You are taken aback by his full black beard, his gentle gray eyes, and his astonishing height. He stretches a foot taller than you! All he is missing is his famous top hat. President Lincoln stares back at you in your all-black getup and diamond-encrusted mask, inquiring calmly, "May I ask who it is that saved my life?"

You have not met the president before this day, but you are familiar with his work. After he issued the Emancipation Proclamation on January 1, 1863, slavery was abolished in the Southern states that seceded from the Union. Black men were permitted to serve in the Union Army and Navy. Although his proclamation did not free *all* slaves throughout the country, the fact that black men could serve in the armed forces was useful to your spy work. Whenever you needed to bring intel to the front lines, you simply disguised yourself as a male soldier. You also know the Gettysburg Address by heart. You are excited to meet the man of many inspiring words and actions. You find your voice, overcoming your starstruck awe.

"I am Mary Bowser, Mr. President," you say, removing your diamond-encrusted mask. "Spy for the Union."

"And what brought you here with such convenient timing, Mary Bowser, Spy for the Union?" asks President Lincoln. If he is astonished by anything about you, he does not show it.

Turn to page 116.

"Right place, right time," you answer. "After spending three long months spying on Confederate President Davis, I have come to work alongside you."

"Let us move to a more acceptable location," suggests President Lincoln, eager to learn more about you and to get away from two bodies on the dirt road.

You follow the president back to the executive mansion where you two discuss your ideas for ending the war and your fresh perspective as a formerly enslaved woman. You go on for hours about improvements that would make the country a better place for all men, women, and former enslaved people. All the while, President Lincoln listens to your suggestions, taking notes and asking questions along the way. You never knew how much you had to say about the state of the nation until you were given the opportunity to voice your opinions.

"I am running for a second term," says President Lincoln once you have finished your fruitful discussion, "and I would be grateful to have a bright, capable individual like you by my side.

"As you saw earlier, things often grow dangerous for me," adds President Lincoln. "It would also help that you know your way around a weapon or two."

"Pointy and I are at your service, sir," you say, playfully putting on the president's top hat. "Let us go win you an election!"

The End

An hour ago, you hopped onto a black stallion named Phoenix and pretended to ride north toward a city in Pennsylvania called Philadelphia. There are new spy recruits there who would benefit from being trained by the great Mary Bowser. Unfortunately for the recruits, however, their training will have to wait.

You never left Richmond, choosing to spy on Bet instead of heading north. You witness firsthand the mistreatment that Bet endures. You watch Bet smile politely when children do not return her greeting. You watch her walk with grace when fellow Virginians shake their heads and call her "crazy," "traitor," and "despicable." You watch Bet hold her head high as townspeople spit at her feet. You had no idea that life in Virginia had gotten so hard for Bet! But, you also watch with pride and wonder as your friend perseveres and carries on about her day despite the bullies that try to lower her to their level.

For nearly two weeks, you follow Bet everywhere she goes. You maintain a safe distance, always watching from a distance. On the twelfth night, the sound of a struggle wakes you from your hiding place, the abandoned shed near Bet's mansion, and run toward Bet's house.

"Never!" hollers Bet. You open the front door and take the stairs two steps at a time. You race to Bet's room on the second floor with Pointy in hand.

Turn to the next page.

Bet's door is wide open. A gray hooded figure stands in front of Bet, holding your friend at sword point. Bet holds her right shoulder, covering a fresh wound.

"Last time," warns the hooded figure in a deep voice, "tell me for whom you work!"

"*Non ducor, duco,*" says Bet in Latin. "I am not led, I lead."

"Wrong answer," says the man, raising the sword to deliver the final blow. You step in front of Bet and hold Pointy up against the sword of the unknown foe. The two swords clang as metal meets metal. You take advantage of the surprise attack, using all your force to send the man backward. He staggers a few steps back. Those steps are enough to knock him off balance and give you the upper hand. You use the man's confusion to strike the weapon from his hand. It falls to the ground. Bet picks up the sword and points it at him.

"He's a Confederate spy," explains Bet, grimacing from the pain of her wounded shoulder. "He came to intimidate me into confessing my allegiance to the Union Army."

"Ah," you say, pulling the handkerchief off your head and giving it to Bet. "That is where you first went wrong, believing that this woman could be intimidated."

"So, tell us," says Bet, tying the handkerchief around her wound. "Who sent *you*?"

The End

"What is going on?" you ask Bet, taking your dear friend's hand. "Why does it sound like you would like me to leave Richmond?"

"I am afraid this city is getting more dangerous for me and that means that you are not safe either," sighs Bet, squeezing your hand. "It has been risky for me to support the Union efforts behind Confederate lines and my actions are costing me a great deal."

"What happened?" you ask, urging Bet to explain.

"Word of my kindness to the 'enemy' has made my life in Virginia impossibly difficult," Bet admits. "I am threatened in the streets because I show sympathy to the Union soldiers. Just yesterday, someone threw a lit torch through my bedroom window! Oh, what has become of my countrymen, Mary? Were we this monstrous before this ugly war?"

"Why did you not mention any of this in our meetings?" you ask, bewildered that all this was happening while you were infiltrating the Confederate White House.

"I needed you to focus," replies Bet, "and I did not want to become one of your missions. I am not a damsel in distress. I will not be made a victim by the very people who used to call me a friend, who used to treat me with kindness, who used to attend my lavish balls and garden parties!"

Go on to the next page.

"Bet, you are a genius!" you say, recalling how respected Bet and the rest of the Van Lews were before the Civil War broke out. Before the war, the Van Lews were a wealthy, dignified family who threw the best parties. People from all over Virginia came to eat, listen to music, and enjoy the Van Lews' company.

"What if we threw a ball?" you ask, hatching a plan to salvage Bet's reputation. "We can frame it as a fundraiser for families displaced by the war!"

"You want to have a party in the middle of a conflict?" asks Bet. "And they call me crazy."

"Think about it," you say, growing more excited with each word. "War has made these men and women forget themselves and who you are. They believe that there are only two sides: themselves and the enemy. What if you blur those lines and convince your fellow Virginians that you are not the traitor that they believe that you are? This ball would remind them that you are the person who once opened your doors to them. Perhaps they would feel less inclined to throw torches into the same home in which they dined and danced."

"It is worth a try," agrees Bet, pulling out a piece of parchment. "I will not be chased from my home, Mary."

"I will not let that happen," you respond. You hand Bet a quill with which to write. "You are like a sister to me. I will not abandon you in your time of need."

"I *am* a sister to you," says Bet, correcting you.

Turn to page 123.

"Okay, that is enough sentiment," you say playfully, helping Bet write down preparations for her ball. "We have a party to plan!"

To your credit, the ball is a major success. Because of your fundraiser, you and Bet are able to bring in food and supplies to families in Virginia who lost loved ones during the war. While the party does not immediately get rid of all the bad blood, it allows Bet to open up a civil line of communication with her fellow Virginians. It is through this line of communication that Bet regains her reputation as a kind, loyal Virginia woman. Of course, Bet does not stop helping the Union cause, but the Virginians never have to know about that.

The End

124

You have waited three months to take down Mr. Eggeling. You stop backpedaling and face him in the shadows. It would be fun to go toe to toe with the insufferable man. Unfortunately, hand-to-hand combat is out of the question. Your challenge is to bring him down without making a single noise. You do not want to wake everyone else in the house and blow your cover. You remain still and silent, watching Mr. Eggeling approach you. When he gets close, you duck behind him and turn him by his shoulders so that he is facing away from you.

"Ahh!" he says as you yank him toward you and wrap your right arm around his neck. You place your other hand around his head and lock your grip, applying pressure.

"Sweet dreams," you whisper to Mr. Eggeling as he goes limp in your arms.

You drag an unconscious Mr. Eggeling back to his room, hoping he will not remember much of your encounter when he awakes in the morning.

With Mr. Eggeling down, you go downstairs to continue your hunt for Arena.

Go on to the next page.

From the window near the front door, you catch a glimpse of movement outside. You squint your eyes, watching a fast-moving figure dressed in white. *Gah!* Arena is getting away!

You pick up the hem of your dress and free your feet from the long, flowing material. You rush from the house, hoping to stop Arena before she gets too deep into the woods. You gain on her as you reach a clearing in the forest near the Confederate White House.

"Ahh!" you yell, lunging forward and tackling Arena to the ground. Arena squirms under your hold, attempting to free herself from your powerful grip.

"I . . . said . . . not . . . another . . . step . . . " you say in between breaths. You are out of breath from taking down Mr. Eggeling and running after Arena. You collect yourself and try again. "Who are you and why did you run?"

"I will tell you who I am," muses Arena, "when you tell me who you are."

"Oh, you are mistaken," you growl, tightening your grip. "I am no longer in the mood to negotiate."

But you are no longer alone—candles begin to flicker at the edge of the forest. With the steward down and you and Arena locked in struggle rather than locked in your bedrooms, you two are likely beyond explanation when you're found out.

The End

126

You make a break for it. You back away from the tall man too quickly. You feel a sense of dread. You are too close to the tall staircase. Your foot snags the soft carpet near the stairs. *Uh oh!* The trip propels you toward the steps! Before you can stop yourself, your momentum gets the best of you. Your body braces for impact as you noisily tumble down each step.

Boom! You instinctively protect your head, tucking your chin down to your chest and placing your arms in front of your face. *Bang!* You turn as you fall, hoping to reduce the injury to your head, face, and arms. *Bam!* You keep your arms and legs bent, rolling into the fall like a crazed armadillo. *Bonk!* You finally land on your right side, colliding with the armchair near the staircase.

You stand up, inspecting your body. Your right side hurts, but you are in one piece. You rub your bruised shoulder, thankful that you have a lot of experience falling. Your trip could have been a lot worse!

"Did you really think that you could get away?" snarls a familiar voice, undermining your small victory.

You look up toward the top of the staircase, meeting the cruel eyes of Mr. Eggeling. Behind him stand President Davis, the First Lady, and several other members of the house. Your *boom, bang, bam,* and *bonk* woke up the entire house. *Gah!* If only you had mastered the art of silently falling down stairs!

The End

The Story of Mary Bowser

When we study and learn about the past, we hope to learn about people of many heritages and backgrounds. But record-keepers of history most often preserved the stories of wealthy people of European backgrounds. This means that what we know to be true about many people in the early United States is incomplete because we do not have good records about the details of their lives. The full life story of Mary Bowser and of many other African Americans, Native Americans, and immigrants who were not of a noble European lineage have sadly not been recorded.

Historical discoveries that change our knowledge are made all the time. Until a discovery reveals more about Mary, we can consider the achievements of her life and her friends through fiction, or invented stories that try to describe her life as best as we can, filling in what we do not know for certain with details we do know about what life was like during the era during which she lived.

More history has been preserved about Mary's friend Elizabeth "Bet" Van Lew, who organized the ring of women who spied for the Union Army during the Civil War. We know that Bet and Mary were lifelong friends, but many other details have been lost. It is possible that Mary's name was Mary Jane Richards, Mary Jane Richards Denman, Mary Jane Richard Garvin, or Mary Bowser. Like many spies, Mary's identity and work were intentionally kept secret.

Bet and Mary grew up together. Mary was born into slavery in the 1830s or 1840s, and was granted freedom as a young child when Bet's father, John Van Lew, died in 1846. Upon his death, Bet and her siblings granted freedom to all of the enslaved people who were part of their household. Bet helped Mary go to school, and she was baptized in 1846.

In 1855, Mary traveled to Liberia in West Africa. She lived there for five years in a missionary community, and returned to Richmond, Virginia, in 1860. In 1861, it is believed that Mary married a man named Wilson Bowser, just as the Civil War began. The Civil War was a devastating, violent war between two parts of the United States, which had gained its independence as a nation less than 100 years before. The main issue at stake was whether to abolish, or outlaw, the practice of slavery by the Southern states.

Tensions between the Northern and Southern states had existed for many years, but the election of Abraham Lincoln in 1860 was the trigger for the Southern states to move to separate, or secede, and form the Confederate States of America. By 1861, the Confederacy declared war on the Union. Mary and Bet lived in Richmond, the Confederate capital, and their allegiance was with the Union Army. They began the dangerous work of spying for the North from their base in the South almost immediately.

Mary and Bet worked together to organize other women in Richmond, the Confederate capitol, to spy for the Union Army. Historians believe Mary did gain entry to President Davis' home as a worker. While undercover in the Davis home, Mary fooled those around her by pretending to be illiterate and unintelligent. She was actually extraordinarily intelligent, with a photographic memory and skills for impersonation. Varina Davis, the First Lady of the Confederacy, was opposed to the war, her beliefs going against her husband and many of those around her.

Mary was also a person guided by incredible passion. She was an excellent public speaker when her true personality—one of confidence—was allowed to shine through. She fought hard for the rights of African American people throughout her whole life.

After the Civil War ended, Mary took on new work as a teacher. In 1867, she founded her own school in Georgia, which had classes for African American adults and children, day and night, weekdays and weekends, hoping to bring education to as many people as possible.

While the recorded history of Mary's life misses many details, we do know she was tremendously brave and smart, and that she and Bet shared a close friendship as they worked to aid the Union Army during the Civil War.

ABOUT THE ARTISTS

Illustrator: Jason Millet is a Chicago-based illustrator who has created storyboards and illustrations for ad agencies, television, children's books, games, and comics. His client list includes Disney, NBC-Universal, DC Comics, Archie Comics, Dark Horse Publishing, and Major League Baseball. His work can be seen in the upcoming *Archie Vs Predator* from Archie/Dark Horse and on the hit TV show *Chicago Fire*.

Cover Artist: Mia Marie Overgaard has been working as a professional artist since graduating from the Royal Danish Academy of Architecture's School of Design in 2006. Mia's creative curiosity has allowed her to span a variety of media and creative fields—from illustration to fashion, graphic design, and fine art. Mia's distinctive illustrations have appeared in numerous books and publications worldwide, and have been exhibited in various locations around the globe such as London, Paris, Estonia, Georgia, Hungary, Sweden, Denmark, and Tokyo.

ABOUT THE AUTHOR

Kyandreia Jones is a Posse Miami Scholar and graduate of Hamilton College where she received her B.A. in Creative Writing. She was born and raised in South Florida. When she thinks of home, she likes to muse that she is in a "sunshine state of mind." Jones' poetry and prose have been published in various college literary publications and magazines such as *Red Weather, Grasping Roots, The Black List Journal,* and *The Underground. Opportunities* like having her first short story "At Home" published by Living Spring Publishers in *Stories Through the Ages, College Edition 2017* inspired Jones' first book *Choose Your Own Adventure SPIES: James Armistead Lafayette.* Working for *Choose Your Own Adventure* has been the highlight of Jones' career and she cannot wait to see what other adventures await her as a writer, visiting author, and public speaker! Jones values reading, writing, laughing, and promoting universal kindness.

For games, activities, and other fun stuff, or to write to Kyandreia, visit us online at CYOA.com

MARY BOWSER TRIVIA QUIZ

1) Mary Bowser is a famous spy. Which of these skills does she NOT use in this book?

❏ Shooting an arrow while standing on the back of a speeding horse

❏ Successfully setting up booby traps to trap people she is spying on

❏ Expert of disguise, hiding in plain sight

2) Who is the bear goddess that visits Mary Bowser?

❏ Rose, the Goddess of Perseverance and Confidence

❏ Trala, the Goddess of Bubbles and Jokes

❏ Bala, the Goddess of Confidence and Fearlessness

3) How does Mary Bowser spy on Jefferson Davis?

❏ By disguising herself as a servant to work in the Confederate White House

❏ By posing as the mail deliverer

❏ By kidnapping the cook

4) Who is Bet Van Lew?

❏ Mary Bowser's friend

❏ The head of the Confederacy

❏ Mary Bowser's archnemesis

5) Where is Abraham Lincoln when Mary Bowser arrives at the presidential mansion to share her ideas?

❏ Taking a nap in his room

❏ He was abducted and taken outside

❏ He was outside watering flowers

6) What job does Mary Bowser have after the Civil War?

❏ Schoolteacher

❏ Postmaster

❏ Horse trainer

Visit us at www.cyoa.com/pages/trivia-quizzes for more questions!

Answers: 1. Successfully setting up booby traps to trap people she is spying on, 2. Bala, the Goddess of Confidence and Fearlessness, 3. By disguising herself as a servant to work in the Confederate White House, 4. Mary Bowser's friend, 5. He was abducted and taken outside, 6. Schoolteacher